OMG...
AM I A
WITCH?!

BY TALIA AIKENS-NUÑEZ

Pinwheel Books

www.pinwheelbooks.com

Library of Congress Control Number: 2013912883
ISBN-13: 978-0-9854248-5-5

TO MY LOVING AND SUPPORTIVE FAMILY

ONE

APRIL tightly held the little, white, fluffy dog as she sat on her bed, her heart pounding so hard, she thought it would pop out of her chest.

"Arrr!" he yelped.

Oh gosh, I'm choking him. She tried to trace the outline of the pink dots on her green blanket, but her hands wouldn't stop shaking. *Breathe. Just breathe. I can't believe I just did that. I can't believe . . . wait—I wonder, what else can I do? Who else can I turn into a dog?*

Her enormous, ugly, fire engine red glasses slid down her face. The sweat that gathered at the tip of her nose dripped onto Austin's head.

"Sorry about that." She wiped the sweat off his cotton ball-looking head, rubbing it farther into his fur. Holding him with one arm, she wiped her clammy hand on the blanket. She switched the dog to the other arm and wiped her other hand.

Breathe in through the nose, out through the mouth—ugh, that yoga class I took with Mom was stupid. She said there would be other girls there my age. Nope, just a bunch of old, deep-breathing moms.

Mrs. Appleton yelled upstairs, "April, is that you?"

Freak! Freak! Did Mom see me run in with Austin? She will kill me! She can't find out about Austin or, my, uh, powers. Wow! I have powers! Would she even be able to tell this is him?

She picked up the dog and took a good look at his face. She wrinkled her nose and shook her head.

"Nope, you look nothing like him. You're smaller than a football. And have more fur than anything else." *I have to fix this ASAP.*

"Grrr . . ." Austin growled.

"Austin, shhhh!" April pleaded, putting her finger over her tightly squeezed lips. "Please, please, please be quiet. I'm trying to figure out what to do. I'm still shocked no one saw you on the bus." She grazed her hand over his head, which was so small it only partly covered her palm.

"Grrr . . ." Austin growled again.

"This is what I get for Googling 'how to turn your brother into a dog.' It actually worked!" April threw her head back and looked at the ceiling. Her eyes filled with tears. "If I just had someone else to ride with on the bus this . . .

★ 3 ★

this . . . this would never have happened." She wished Grace had been there to ride home with. April continued to pet Austin. She knew he understood her.

The soft fur brushing against her hand soothed her. "If I knew that new girl, Eve, a little better I would have sat with her instead of—" She looked down at him. He narrowed his eyes at her. Her hand dropped to the comforter.

"Sorry, Austin," she sighed. "We just have to sneak downstairs to the computer without Mom seeing us. And, I can Google 'how to undo turning your pestering brother into a dog.'"

"Grrr . . ."

"Well, it is sort of *your* fault this happened."

"Grrr . . ."

"Well, fine. Maybe no one really deserves to be, you know, turned into a dog, but . . . but, you are soooo mean and annoying."

Austin grumbled. He turned his head away from her. She ignored him.

"OK. Well, how about I text Grace and ask her to do the search? She has a computer in her room."

Click-clack. Click-clack. The steps got closer. The sound grew louder. *Click-Clack. Click-CLACK.* Her heart raced as she heard each step.

"April, are you home?" her mother yelled up the stairs.

"Yes, Mom!" April yelled through the closed door.

"Is Austin home, too?"

April held her breath as if that would stop time. Her heart pounded so hard she felt it in her head.

"Uh . . . I think he . . . uh . . . had practice?"

Tell her more so that she doesn't try to find him. Think fast. Think fast.

"I don't know what he's doing." She took a deep breath again. "But, uh, he said he would be home later. And, to tell you not to worry . . . or call . . . he'll be home."

OMG! I have never ever lied to her! I am a horrible daughter. But, her mother couldn't know about Austin. She would be so mad at April if she knew she had turned him into a dog. *WOW! Did I really just do that? Did I really just turn my brother into a dog* and *lie to my mother in the same hour?*

Click-CLACK. Click-clack. Her mom returned to the living room.

April let out a huge breath. "Geez, that was bad."

Austin grunted as if he agreed.

"Thanks, Austin . . ." She straightened her back and squeezed her shoulder blades together, looking down at him under her glasses. "Even though you are a year older than me, I kind of like feeling . . . bigger and . . ." she cleared her throat, "witch-ier!"

"Grrrr . . ."

"Well, too bad *I'm* the witch and you're the dog."

Am I really a witch?

TWO

APRIL had always been curious. Three years ago, when April was in the second grade, she had discovered she could search for answers to her questions online. She was excited by her new discovery of Google. But, that is how she had gotten herself into this mess. *What does all of this mean? What else can I do? What will happen if people, the wrong people, find out about my, uh, powers?*

She put Austin between her elbow and body.

With one hand, she unzipped her book bag and grabbed her phone. As fast as her fingers could move, she texted Grace: OMG . . . I may be a witch?!

Within seconds, Grace texted back: HA HA VERY FUNNY . . .

April texted: I'm not kidding! Can U Google 4 me how 2 undo spell that turned ur brother into a dog?

Her phone quickly rang.

She answered it. "OMG Grace! I don't know what to do! We need to Google how to fix this!"

"Well . . . what happened?" Grace asked. "You turned Austin into a dog? *Really*? And, can you also morph into a werewolf? Then into a mouse?"

April felt her body tighten as her breath quickened.

"Arrr!" Austin yelped.

"Oh sorry, Austin. I—"

★ 9 ★

"OMG! Who was that? Was that who, or what, I think it is?"

"Yep," April answered in a low voice. She cleared her throat. "Definitely a dog. I, um, squeezed him a little too hard."

"You HAVE to get over here. STAT." Grace watched too many doctor television shows. She liked using their lingo.

"You can't tell anyone!" said April. "I mean, *no one* else can know. Ok?"

Silence.

"Hello Grace? Are you there?"

"Uh huh, just busy pinching myself to make sure this isn't a dream."

"Or nightmare. I can't believe I just turned my annoying brother into a dog. I mean he deserved it. Well, sorta. I feel even more horrible because I had to lie to my mom."

"Breathe, April. I do have to say, you were

quite clever to be able to sneak him off the bus and into your house with no one seeing you."

April straightened her back and smirked. "I guess you're right. I am pretty clever."

"April, just come over so we can try to figure this out. It will be easier for us to Google over here since I have a computer in my room. At your house, we would have to sneak downstairs and do it with a parent over our shoulders. Right?"

"Yeah. You're right. See you in a little while."

"April, I can see your house from my window," Grace laughed.

"You're right again. See you in a minute." April exhaled hard and dropped the phone on her bed.

Holding Austin and his mouth shut with one arm, she walked to the door and opened it. He wiggled his body, pressing his paws into her side.

"Arrr . . ."

"Sorry, I didn't realize I squeezed that hard," she whispered to him.

She gently placed each foot in front of the other. Her hand grasped the railing. She peered down the stairs. Like a penny to a magnet, she found her mother's voice.

All clear. Go for it. She's yapping on the phone again.

The words became louder.

April's heart started to beat faster. She quickly backed up, bumping Austin's tail on doorway to her room. "Grrr . . ."

"Sorry," she whispered. "But be quiet, or I'll do it again—harder."

Should she leave Austin here? *No. I need to find a way to get him out of the house with me.* She looked around her room and froze as she saw her book bag. *Perfect. I'll put him in that.*

He wiggled. She held him tighter. Using one

of his front paws, Austin tried to push April's hand off his mouth. With her free hand, she took her weekend homework, notebooks, and books out of the book bag. She stuffed Austin and her cell phone into it.

"You'd better be quiet—or else."

Austin whimpered. He looked so cute and fluffy. She kissed his head. "I'm sorry, Austin." Beads of sweat formed on her nose, causing her ugly red glasses to slide down. She pushed them back into place. "I would never do anything like this to anyone but, but—you pushed me!"

Austin moved his back legs, raising himself higher out of the book bag.

"You were picking on me, as *usual*. You just didn't expect me to fight back this time, did you?"

Scratch, scratch, scratch.

"Stop trying to get out the bag. We have to get to Grace's. Do you want to be a dog forever?

If you don't stop, I'll use my witch powers and do something worse to you."

His eyes grew larger. His movements stopped. He slowly sat down.

Maybe I really am a witch. I can get the Prankster of the Year to listen to me.

She zipped up the book bag, put it on, and ran down the stairs. She reached for the front doorknob. Frozen, with her hand on the knob, she looked into the kitchen.

"Mom, can I go to Grace's house?"

"Hold on one second . . ." April's mom said as she put the phone down and came toward her.

Oh no! Is she going to say no? Please don't open my book bag. Then I will have to explain. She will soooo kill me!

THREE

"**I**F **YOUR** brother is hanging out with Michael, tell him to give me a—" *AHCHOO!* Mrs. Appleton covered her nose.

"Bless you," said April.

Oh no. I have to get Austin away from her. This is why she said we can't have a dog— SHE'S ALLERGIC!!! OMG! OMG! This being-a-witch stuff is super hard.

April started nervously tapping her foot.

"Thank you. Uh . . . tell him to call me," Mrs. Appleton said.

"Grrr . . ."

Austin, be quiet.

April reached her arm around, under the backpack, to her shoulder, acting as if she were scratching her back. The backpack shifted and tossed Austin around.

"OK, Mom, I love you." April grasped the doorknob and turned.

"Do you have to go to the bathroom?" April's mom asked, looking at her tapping foot.

"No." April stopped tapping. "I just, um, wanted to go hang out with Grace, you know?"

Her mother's frown turned into a smile. Mrs. Appleton leaned in to give April a kiss on her forehead and *AHCHOO!*

"Ewww . . . great . . . a Friday afternoon shower." April wiped her face and forehead.

My mother just sneezed on me. Gross! She had to get this dog out of there before her mom got worse. *Geez, I don't want to make her sick.*

"Sorry, honey. Have fun with Grace."

"GRRR . . ."

"April, did you hear that?" April's mom looked at the backpack. April quickly shifted from one foot to the other, tossing Austin around again.

"No . . . Nope, didn't hear anything. Uh, OK, Mom . . . see you later."

April opened the door and jumped down the two steps right outside the front door. Her mother followed, stopping at the doorway.

Mrs. Appleton looked at the ground outside the door and around the bushes on both sides. "I don't see anything," she said. "I wonder where that noise came from . . ."

April briskly walked away.

"The tissues are on the dining room table," April said as she reached the end of the path and turned onto the sidewalk. Out of the corner of her eye, she watched her mother search the ground outside the house.

She looks okay. I had to get him out of there as fast as I could. She remembered the time her mother had an allergy attack from being around Uncle Jim's two dogs. Her eyes swelled shut. Her father had to rush to the pharmacy to get her some allergy tablets. *Geez, I felt badly for her then . . . and I wasn't even the cause of it. Now, I am.*

She looked back and saw her mom go back inside. She bit her lip as she walked to Grace's house. *I will never lie to her again.*

FOUR

GRACE opened the door before April could knock on it. She grabbed April's arm, pulled her inside, and led her up the stairs past her brother's room.

"Mom!" Grace yelled. "April and I are going to do some research online for our essay on the president."

"That's fine, girls," Mrs. Galapagos said from the next room.

When they reached her room, Grace closed

the door. She whipped her head around to meet April's eyes. "What did you do? WHAT happened?"

April looked down at the bright blue carpet. As she lifted her head, she admired the clouds and sky painted on the walls. All she could imagine was floating off into the clouds. Or flying to the stars on the other wall. She fixated on the big yellow sun behind Grace's bed.

Grace waved her hand in front of April's face. "Earth to April . . ."

April dropped her arms. The book bag slid down her back and landed on the ground. Swallowing the lump in her throat, she unzipped it and took out the dog.

Grace's jaw dropped. "Is that . . ."

April nodded.

"No way! Prove it!"

"How? I'm not the Dog Whisperer."

Grace looked at Austin. "Wag your tail when

I say my brother's name. Justin . . . David . . . Aaron . . . Michael—"

"Arf," Austin yelped and wagged his tail.

Grace's jaw dropped and her eyes bulged.

"Hello, Grace? You ok?"

"Well, I guess this is Austin." Grace looked into the little white dog's eyes. She squeezed her eyebrows together. "How did this happen? When did it happen? And how come I didn't know you could do this kind of . . . stuff?"

"I really didn't mean to! I was mad one day last week so I searched online 'how to turn someone into a dog.' I found a spell book. I think it was called *The Book of Magic* or something like that." April shrugged her shoulders. "I didn't know that I even remembered the spell until Austin was bugging me on the bus today. I warned him. I told him if he didn't stop bothering me, I would turn him into a dog. He didn't believe me. So I . . . uh . . . proved it?"

FIVE

"WHOA, whoa, April. Let's start from the beginning." Grace took a few deep breaths, and slowly sat on the chair in front of her computer. Her eyes stayed glued on the dog. "I'm scared to ask, BUT what happened on the bus? The one day I go to the doctor I miss all the good stuff."

"So, Austin sat next to me—" April started.

"OK. That's not a crime." Grace threw her hands up in the air.

April rolled her eyes. "I know. Let me finish."

"Sorry . . ."

"You know I broke my glasses last week. That's why I'm wearing these huge ugly red ones. I mean, seriously, what other fifth grader has big red glasses?"

"You're right! NO ONE else does," Grace agreed. "They kinda look like red hula hoops."

"Thanks, Grace."

Austin let out a little whimper, which almost sounded like a laugh.

"Seriously? You're a dog. How can you laugh?" April flopped onto the bed. Her feet just touched the carpet. "So . . . he said, 'Hey, Awkward Appleton, can you see the ants on the ground outside the bus—since you're wearing magnifying glasses?'" April made her voice deeper and lifted her shoulders, trying to mimic Austin.

Austin let out another little laughing whimper.

Grace shot Austin a cold glare.

"Then he started making fun of my braces, calling me 'metal mouth' and 'brace face.'" She looked down at her hands.

"That is SOOO mean!" Grace said, quickly moving her eyes from April to Austin. Austin groaned and turned his head away.

"AND, this morning he only left me crumbs in the cereal box . . . on purpose. He had two bowls of cereal and only left a few drops of milk! I had to eat oatmeal with water. He knows I hate oatmeal, and I hate it even more with water."

"Geez! Older brothers are so annoying. But you're luckier than me. You could have Michael as an older brother. The other day he came into my room, farted, then ran right back to his room." Grace wrinkled up her nose.

"EWWW! That's gross. I guess you're right. It could be worse. When Austin and I were younger, we played together a lot. And, that was fun . . . *then*," April said, glaring at the dog. "He's become such a mean pain in the butt. Remember last week?"

"What? I forget . . ."

"He asked me if I wanted to do an art project. I said 'yes.' You know I love art. It's my fave." April took a deep breath.

"He gave me a plain white t-shirt and asked me to put it on. I thought—stupid me—he was spray painting on the back or something. He told me to lie straight back on a sheet of white paper he said he put on the rug. I didn't check—stupid me. He told me it was a new technique he learned in art class. I tried to turn around to look at the paper. But he told me if I moved too much I might mess up the picture he painted on the shirt. So, I lay straight back. He pulled my hair, said 'I'm the Prankster of the Year.' Then he ran away. When I tried to get up, I couldn't. I was stuck to the rug! He covered my back with instant dry glue. There was no paper. It was so traumatizing!"

"Oh my . . ." Grace covered her mouth with her hand.

April looked down at the rug, wringing her hands. "My mom had to come get me. She helped me slide out of the shirt. She had to use paint thinner to get the shirt off the rug. He got in a lot of trouble, but I felt like such a nothing. That's when I Googled that spell," April said. "But I never, ever imagined it would work, let alone in the school bus! I just thought of the spell in my head and . . . poof! It happened! I'm just glad nobody noticed and I was able to sneak him quickly into my backpack."

Grace put her face right in front of Austin's.

"Well, maybe now you'll stop playing jokes on April."

"Grrr . . ."

Bam!

April and Grace stared at each other without blinking. They turned to the closed bedroom door.

"Hello? Anyone home?" Mr. Galapagos called.

Grace turned to the computer and started typing super fast. "We'll have to talk about this more later. We need to start searching NOW."

SIX

"**H**ELLO?" Grace's dad said cheerfully. They heard Grace's mom and dad talking. Then, there was a long pause.

"Ugh, April! I think they're kissing," Grace said, grabbing her stomach.

"So annoying. My parents do that, too."

"Gross." They said at the same time. They both laughed.

"Michael! Grace! Kids, are you home?" They

heard footsteps coming up the stairs.

"Oh no, Grace! He's coming upstairs," April said, trying to whisper.

"Quick! We have to find a place to hide Austin. I know my dad will ask a ton of questions, and, and, and—"

They both jumped up. April's body shook from the fear that Mr. Galapagos could find Austin—as a dog.

She ran around the room, looking in every corner.

Grace walked right to her closet door and yanked it open. She picked up something from the floor. "This is the purse I had from Aunt Mary's wedding a few years ago."

"Oh, it's so pretty. Your dress was purple and shiny like that too, right?"

Grace unzipped it and dumped her lip-glosses on the closet floor. "Yep."

April held Austin with both hands. She turned his face to hers. The beating of her heart slowed. Staring at his wide eyes reminded her of her brother years ago—when he was nice.

She whispered in his ear, "Please be quiet. I am begging you." She stuffed him into the purse. Grace zipped it back up and dropped him on the closet floor.

"Arrr . . ."

April kneeled down on the floor. Hovering over the purse, she whispered, "Shhhh, Austin. But, uh, sorry about that." She glanced up at all of Grace's clothes hanging perfectly in the closet, as the steps grew louder and closer. Hopping to her feet, she closed the closet door.

"He's coming," Grace said in a hushed voice.

Tippy-toe, tippy-toe, tippy-toe. Flop. April landed on Grace's bed, kicked off her shoes, and crossed her legs. Grace slid back into the desk chair, and started typing, P-R-E-S-I-D-E-N-T.

"Hi, girls," Mr. Galapagos said, smiling as he opened the door. His smile went away and he tilted his head to the side. "April, why are you sweating? Are you okay?"

"Uh . . ." Grace jumped in.

Say school lunch, thought April. *I'm sick from school lunch. No, don't say that. That would get me a trip to the doctor. Or even worse, a trip to the hospital. Say something. What else . . .*

"We did relay races at school. So, I am . . . uh . . . hot and tired," April said, staring at the closet door.

"Oh, okay," he said, raising one eyebrow. "Are you staying for dinner, April?"

"Ummm . . ." April said, still staring at the closet. Grace's dad looked at the closet door.

Grace kicked April.

Ouch! Ok, now stop staring at the closet. April looked at Mr. Galapagos. *Breathe. Say something . . . say anything.*

SEVEN

"WE WERE just about to call her mom now," Grace said, reaching into April's book bag for her cell phone, and then waving it. "Can you ask Mom if it's okay?"

"Sure, Honey Bear."

"Dad!"

He jerked his head to look at Grace. "Sorry. I forgot you're in middle school and not my Honey Bear anymore." He walked over to Grace and gave her a kiss on her forehead. "Well ladies, we will order enough pizza. But April . . ." Mr. Galapagos glanced at the closet door again.

Oh no. He knows something. Oh no!

"April, just rest up before dinner."

"Thank you, Mr. Galapagos." *Breathe before you turn purple. Whew!*

He looked at his watch, then the computer screen. "Oh. I have to go get your brother soon. You kids finish working on your essay." He walked out of Grace's room and left the door open. "Honey, need help cleaning up?" he yelled to Grace's mom.

"Whew!" Grace exhaled. "He's gone."

"That was close," April whispered, listening to Mr. Galapagos walk down the stairs.

"We have to work fast," April said, stretching her legs out on Grace's bed. "Where were we?"

"I am searching for a spell breaker. Remember?" Grace turned to the computer and started typing. "You said you found it in *The Book of Magic*, right?"

"Oh yeah, oops. Let me get Austin." April sprang to her feet and opened the closet door. She looked down at the purple purse on the ground. It had landed in the only empty space among the perfectly paired shoes. He wiggled back and forth in the purse. She picked it up and opened it.

Austin shoved his nose out.

"Grrr . . ." He growled and showed his teeth.

"You didn't bark or say anything." April hugged him and gave him a big kiss on the head. "Thank you, Austin!" He grumbled at her. "Oh stop it," she scolded. She looked at his wide brown eyes.

Why does he look so scared? He was always such a tough guy. But, is he scared now?

She relaxed her hand, not holding him so tightly.

"Are you afraid?"

"Grrrr . . ." Then, he attempted to wiggle out of the purse as if he were trying to run away.

"Austin, if you don't stop, I'm going to put you back in the purse."

She took him out and pinned him between her elbow and her body again. She gently scratched him under his chin and sat on Grace's bed.

"I can't find anything," Grace said as she turned to look at April.

"Really?" April peered over Grace's shoulder at the computer screen.

"Is that the dog breathing on my neck or you? Ewww." Grace said, standing up from the computer chair.

"Fail." April smirked at Grace.

"OK genius. Fine. You give it a try." Grace took Austin from April's arms.

April sat down and typed "*Book of Magic* spell to reverse turning someone into a dog." She pressed 'Enter.'

Click. Click.

"Here it is!" April pointed to the screen.

"Seriously? Seriously?" Grace dropped Austin on the bed. She hovered over April, looking at the computer screen. "I searched those exact same keywords and I didn't get anything. Hmmm . . . Maybe it's because I'm *not* a witch so I, uh, couldn't find it."

April stopped breathing, fixated on Grace's eyes. Just as she took a breath, Austin jumped off the bed and ran out Grace's door.

EIGHT

THEY watched Austin's little tail wiggle as he ran through the door and down the hall.

April screamed, "Ahhh!"

She ran to the doorway. Austin ran past the linen closet, past Grace's parents' bedroom, past the bathroom, and into Michael's room.

Grace's mother yelled up the stairs, "Everything OK?"

"Oh yeah, it's fine, Mom," said Grace. "We . . .

uh . . . thought we saw a bug. But it . . . wasn't. Sorry!"

"OK, girls," she said, going back into the kitchen.

"Oh no," Grace whispered. "Michael's room is so junky. I have no clue where he went in that pigsty."

"Oh, Austin's room is a disaster, too." April nodded. "Austin should feel right at home in there."

They heard footsteps walking toward the front door.

"Rita, I'll be right back. I'm going to get him now and pick up the pizzas," Grace's dad said to her mom. The front door closed.

"Oh no!" they said at the same time.

"Michael will be here soon," Grace said, her eyes growing as big as a high school girl's hoop earrings.

April felt the blood rush to her cheeks. Beads of sweat formed on Grace's forehead. They tiptoed down the hall into Michael's room.

April's eyes bulged. "How in the world can he even tell what is clean and what is dirty? I guess it's all dirty. There has gotta be mold or a fungus growing somewhere in here."

A cracked bat was wedged between underwear and a grass stained white t-shirt on the floor. Books sat piled in the corner with what looked like a granola bar wrapper peeking out from underneath a book cover. In the other corner was what appeared to be a pile of dirt but were actually dirt-covered track sneakers. His walls were covered with posters of famous athletes.

"It smells like a locker room mixed with a school cafeteria," April said, wrinkling her nose.

"I think there's actually a picture of a

baseball, basketball, and football on this rug," Grace said quietly.

"There's a rug under here?"

Grace rolled her eyes. "I know. Hard to believe."

"Where would a little dog hide in this room?" April asked. "Austin, I know you're mad at me. Heck, I would be mad at me, too, but, but seriously." She stamped her foot, but lightly so as not to alert Mrs. Galapagos. "Seriously, please come out so we can fix this." April let out a huge sigh.

Grace got down onto her hands and knees, slowly lifted the blanket hanging from the bed, and looked under it. "Some dirty clothes and socks." She reached under the bed and pulled something out, holding it with two fingers. With her other hand, she pinched her nose.

"Ewww. I guess that sock used to be white," April said.

"This is gross." Grace dropped the sock to the floor and stood up. "Your turn . . ."

April got down and crawled around the floor on her hands and knees.

Austin is always so annoying. Why won't he just come out so we can try to fix this? What if we can't find him? What if we get caught?

Her breath quickened. She looked under Michael's desk.

"Nope, only an old bag of Doritos." She looked under his dresser. "Nothing but lots of lint and dust." April threw her body back and flopped onto her butt. She put her head in her hands and swallowed hard. "This is hopeless!"

"We have to find him fast," Grace said, pacing and biting her lip. "My dad will be home soon with Michael."

April stood up. "I know." She cleared her throat, fighting back the tears. "And, we don't want to tell Michael about all of this. He'd get us in so much trouble—because you know how he loves to try to get us in trouble."

Grace closed Michael's door. "Austin?" she said quietly. "We found the spell to fix this. If you come out, hopefully we can do it—"

"Austin, I will do anything you want," April interrupted. "I am sooooo sorry!" She started to cry, wetting her glasses with tears. She took them off and wiped them with her shirt. "Gosh, not only did I turn my brother into a dog, *now* I lost him." Out of the corner of her eye, she saw Austin stick his head out of Michael's closet. April jumped on Austin and hugged him. She squeezed him so tightly he let out a little yelp.

"Chillax, April," said Grace. "Chillax."

"Sorry, Austin. I didn't realize my strength," April said with a chuckle. She stood up, still hugging him.

NINE

APRIL was overjoyed that she had found Austin. She was still hugging him.

Grace came over and gave Austin a kiss on his head. She looked up at April as if she smelled sour milk. "Ewww. I just kissed your brother."

April laughed and kissed him on the head, too. Austin grumbled but gently rubbed his nose against April's hand. April kissed him again. She felt her cheeks tremble from her big, broad smile.

"We'd better get out of here before Michael gets home," Grace said, opening the door.

They did a running tiptoe down the hall back into Grace's room. April quietly closed the door behind them. Grace ran to the computer, sat, and started clicking.

April sat on the bed holding Austin and started to pet him. He growled again. She knew he was growling at her for treating him like a little doggie. She smiled because she felt as if things would go back to the way they had been. Austin would go back to being an annoying brother and she would have nice new glasses again.

"Now where were we?" April asked.

"April? Are you serious? Remember, the spell breaker?" Grace said.

"Oh, yeah."

"I wonder how many people can get to this book," Grace said, her eyes glued to the computer screen.

"Right, are there other witches out there?" April asked, looking into space. "I wonder who else can do this kind of, uh, stuff."

Grace's eyes bulged as she started reading. "April, put Austin in the closet and close the door."

April placed Austin on the closet floor as nicely as she could. Austin sighed and lay down. April gently closed the door.

"Now repeat after me," Grace said.

"Heaven, please help with the recent past,
To undo the spell that I just cast.
Please take this request as formal,
And turn my brother back to normal."

April repeated each line as Grace said it.

"Did it—" Grace swallowed, "did it work?" She looked at the closet door.

"I'm scared to open it," said April.

Grace raised her shoulders. "Why?"

"Well, what if it didn't work?" April's eyes burned as they filled with tears.

Grace stood up and gave her a hug. "Don't cry. If it didn't work, we'll . . . we'll figure it out. But, the only way to know if we have to keep searching is if you open the door. It might have worked."

"But . . ." April cleared her throat.

"Just open the door! For the love of God."

April turned to face the closet. She stared at it. She could not move.

"Did I tell you about the time Miss Meanie gave me detention for talking in class? Jimmie was in detention, too—as usual. He's such a troublemaker. He threw spitballs and paper clips at me when she wasn't looking. I told Austin how mean Jimmie was to me. I don't know what he said to Jimmie. But, the next day, Jimmie said sorry to me." April swallowed hard.

"Austin always bothered me," she said, staring at the closet door. "But he was a good big brother. He didn't let anyone else pick on me."

"Did you just say Austin *was* a good big brother?" asked Grace. "April, if this doesn't, work we WILL figure it out. Geez, we are, like, two of the smartest girls in school."

"You're right. Ok—"

"Maybe I would like Michael more if I turned him into a dog," Grace said, staring into space.

April's heart beat faster and her breaths quickened. She reached for the knob and, with her eyes tightly shut, turned it very slowly. Then she slowly cracked one eye. She opened the door slower than a slug crosses the sidewalk.

Her heart sank. The little white dog stared sadly at April.

TEN

AUSTIN'S glassy eyes looked so sad. April sighed as Austin hung his head. She collapsed to her knees to get closer to him.

"It didn't work." She picked Austin up and held him with both hands. "I'm sorry, Austin," she whispered in his ear. She kissed his head, and the lump in her throat grew bigger and bigger.

Swallowing hard, she dropped onto the bed, tears falling from her eyes.

Her glasses were dripping, and her tears wet Austin's head. She put him on the bed. He lay down with a sigh, turned his head away, and covered his face with his paws. She dried her glasses with her shirt.

What have I done? I'm such a super horrible sister. How come it didn't work? Why can I make some things happen but not this one little—well not so little—thing happen? What if I never get him back?

Grace's eyes darted from the open closet door to the window to the bedroom door. She was feverishly tapping a pen on her desk. She always had that focused look when she was thinking hard about something.

"Oops. I forgot to close that closet door," April said, putting her glasses back on.

BAM! The closet door slammed shut. April held her breath. She and Grace looked at each other. Neither of them blinked.

"What! What just happened?" Grace whispered.

"OMG . . . oh my . . . that keeps happening." April looked down at the ground. *Geez, I thought me turning on the fan by just thinking about it the other day was just a fluke.*

"What do you mean 'that'?" Grace asked, using her fingers as quotation marks.

"I keep thinking about something small . . . like . . . like turning on the fan or closing the door. Then, poof! The door closed on its own. You saw it . . ."

Grace took a deep breath. "April, I have an idea. But you have to trust me."

April stared at Grace. "Ok."

"You know the new girl in school, Eve?" Grace asked.

"Yeah. Eve LaRue, right? She rides our bus. Eve was a few rows away from Austin and me this afternoon."

"She may be able to help us."

"How?" April raised one eyebrow.

"Well, she told me something," Grace whispered. "Remember, that day last week when you were sick? I ate lunch with Eve. I asked her where she was from. She said Nor Leans, Louisiana. She said her dad got a new job, so that's why they moved up here."

"I wish you would have introduced us before," said April. "Then, I would have sat with her on the bus. And, NONE of this would have happened. Austin wouldn't have been making fun of my glasses, I wouldn't be thinking about maybe being a witch, and I wouldn't be freaking out about my mom and dad finding me with Austin—who's a DOG!"

"Chillax, April. Try to—"

"Sorry. I am trying to chill out and relax." April threw her head back and let out a loud sigh.

"So . . ." Grace continued, "when I got home, I was bored. I searched online about Nor Leans, Louisiana. I found out that a lot of French people live there. And it has a weird spelling N-E-W O-R-L-E-A-N-S."

April smiled. "Thanks for the social studies report."

"AND," Grace continued, "a lot of witches live there."

April rolled her eyes and jumped off the bed. "Boy, you can tell long stories," she mumbled under her breath. She started playing with the nose of one of the teddy bears sitting on top of Grace's bookshelf. He was brown. His fur was mostly soft with a few spots. He looked as if she had fallen asleep on him a few times with her mouth open.

"So, the next day at gym," Grace continued, "I asked Eve about New Orleans and I told her about what I found online. Then, Eve whispered in my ear that her grandma was a witch doctor."

"Really!" April looked at Grace, wide-eyed in amazement.

Grace nodded. "Yep."

"OK?" April stopped walking around her room and shrugged. "So, how does that help us now? What should I do?"

ELEVEN

"NADA." Grace was taking Spanish this year. She tried to use it every day. "Let's call Eve and ask her what to do. After gym, I got her number so we could hang out sometime, maybe to come over to paint nails and watch movies, like we always do."

Grace dialed. She put the phone on speaker.

"Hello?" said a girl's voice.

Grace turned the volume down on her phone. "Hello, may I speak to Eve?"

"This is she."

"Hi, Eve. This is Grace . . . from school. Remember me?"

"Oh, yeah. How you doin'?"

"I'm good. I'm calling with my friend April. She also goes to school—"

"Arf." Austin let out a quiet bark.

"Austin, be quiet," April said, trying to muzzle him. He growled.

"Do you have a puppy?" Eve asked.

"Well, uh, that is why we are calling you." Grace swallowed. "Remember how you told me about your grandmother? Well, April sort of turned her brother into a dog."

"Oh my!" Eve gasped. "How did you do that? Was it your fairy godmother?" She chuckled.

April's hands started to shake. A lump grew in her throat. "Well . . . I found this spell online that I, um, tried and poof! It worked." She swallowed. "Since your grandma was a witch healer we thought maybe you could help us—"

"Wow." Eve sounded amazed. "Maybe you have 'the gift.' And, I reckon you mean 'witch doctor.'" She laughed. "Yeah, I'll help ya'll out." She had a little accent.

"Thank you, Eve!" April said happily. "But what is 'the gift'?"

"So, April, my *grand-mère* was a witch doctor," Eve said.

"Your . . . who?" April asked, scratching her head.

"I should explain. *Grand-mère* is 'grandma' in French. Many people in my family speak French."

"Remember, April? I told you a lot of French people live in New Orleans!" Grace said.

"I get that. I'm not *that* slow. Eve just seems so . . . uh . . . normal and . . . well the witch doctors I've seen in movies—"

Eve laughed. "Movies also have talking animals." The girls laughed. Austin's groan sounded like a laugh. The girls laughed harder.

"So, my *grand-mère* has a spell book," Eve said. "I found it one day. My mom sent me down to the gross basement. It's dark and . . . ewww! Anyway, April, my *grand-mère* said if you can do spells, then you have a gift."

"WHAT?" April shrugged her shoulders.

"She said gifts can be fun and exciting, but they also bring a lot of responsibility," Eve said. "And, if you are not careful, they can bring big problems. But, that the universe gives us all blessings. This may be a gift you have."

"So, my gift may be that I am a witch?"

TWELVE

"**Y**EP. You may be a witch. So you can do spells like this one," Eve said.

"OH NO! OH NO!!! I will NEVER do anything like this again. I've learned my lesson," April said, staring at Austin. "I like experiments. BUT, I kind of . . . uh . . . miss my brother. I won't say those words EVER again. AND, I'm scared about what Mom and Dad might do to me if they find out."

"Well, let's meet here tomorrow morning.

Eve, can you bring your spell book?" Grace asked.

"Yes ma'am," Eve said with her polite Southern accent.

Grace looked at April. "Actually, let's meet at April's house, since my brother will be here."

"Good idea, Genius Galapagos," April chimed in.

"OK," said Eve, "I'll be over in the morning with the spell book."

"Arf," Austin quietly barked.

"Perfect. I guess Austin agrees, too," April said, sitting back down on the bed. She tucked Austin under her arm.

The girls laughed.

"Oh NO!" She jumped off the bed again.

"April, what's wrong?" Grace asked.

She pointed to the clock "Look! It's already five o'clock."

"Uh oh," Grace said. "Oh my gosh! Austin is

supposed to get out of practice soon . . . in less than an hour."

"We don't have much time," April said as the blood rushed to her face.

"How are you going to get through tonight . . . with Austin . . . as a dog?"

"Oh! I have an idea," Eve said.

"Please share. We need all the help we can get," Grace said, looking at the clock.

"Your brothers are best friends, too, right?"

"Yes," they replied together.

"Grace, ask your mother if April can sleepover. Then get your mother's cell phone and text April's mom, asking if both April and Austin can sleepover. That will get you time until tomorrow. You just have to hide Austin tonight."

April and Grace exhaled. Grace's smile grew bigger and bigger. "I know just how we can do it."

"Eve, you are SUPER smart!" April said, grinning. "Tomorrow, we will turn Austin from white and fluffy to brown haired and scruffy. I hope." She tried to keep the smile on her face. "Eve, we will see you tomorrow morning. Be here early, ok?"

"Yes ma'am," Eve said. "See ya'll in the morning."

They hung up.

Grace quickly moved her eyes to meet April's. "OK . . . here's the plan . . . I'll go down-stairs and ask my mom if you can sleepover. You come downstairs and go into the dining room. She leaves her purse on the table, and she keeps her cell phone in the side pocket. Grab it. Then, we'll come upstairs. Sound good?"

"But, what do we do with Austin?" April asked, looking at the little white dog.

He looks so sad and depressed, she thought. *I don't think he has lain still like this since . . .*

well . . . ever! I am such a horrible sister. What kind of sister turns their brother into a dog? I can't believe I got myself into this mess.

"Let's put him back in the closet," Grace said.

April gently placed him on the closet floor, giving him a farewell pat on the head. "I'll be right back." She stood up. "Oh geez!" she said as she grabbed Grace's trashcan. She started digging through it, taking out all the used paper and napkins.

Grace's eyes bulged. "WHAT are you doing?"

April shooed the shoes out of the front corner of the closet. She feverishly flattened the papers on top of each other and placed them in the corner. "Just in case he has to go potty: a little wee-wee pad."

As April closed the closet door, leaned her back against it, and stared off into the distance.

OMG! This REALLY could backfire on me. What if my parents find out? I would never— and I mean NEVER—see the light of day again. Forget sleepovers. Forget dances. Forget ever learning to drive. Forget life . . .

April blinked hard. She took the phone from Grace and started texting her mother.

THIRTEEN

"I'M GOING to ask if I can stay over to eat pizza and sleep over," April told Grace as she typed out the text message. "So, when we text from your mom's phone, my mom will just say, 'Yeah, sure.'"

"Oh. Good idea," Grace said as they sat on the edge of her bed.

"Mom," April said aloud as she was texting, "can I stay at Grace's house for pizza? And, can I sleep over? Thx." She hit *send.*

"Now we have to go downstairs and get my mother's phone," said Grace. "Do you remember what I told you?"

April was still looking at the phone's screen. "'Bout what?"

"Hello? Earth to April . . . About where the phone is?"

Gosh. First, I lied to my mother. Now I'm planning to steal Mrs. Galapagos's phone. April lifted her head and fixed her glasses. "Oh, yeah. On the dining room table . . . in her purse, right?"

"Yeah."

"Who knew I'd be getting quizzed over here?" April said, rolling her eyes.

"Come on." Grace grabbed April's hand and pulled her to the door. April left the phone on Grace's bed.

They tiptoed down the stairs. One stair, two stairs, three stairs . . . *creak. Creak! CREAK!*

"Shhh," Grace said quietly, her finger over her mouth.

"I'm trying. You're being loud, too."

"Hello? Girls?" Grace's mom called. They could hear Mrs. Galapagos's steps getting closer to the stairs.

"Come on," April said, walking faster.

She has to stay in the kitchen. If she stays in the kitchen, she can't see me digging through her purse on the dining room table. She would have to walk really close to the doorway to see me digging through her bag. April's stomach churned and did flips.

They reached the bottom of the stairs. April's heart thumped so loudly she put her hand on it, hoping that would slow it down. Grace turned as her mom passed through the kitchen doorway, and quickly walked to meet her mother before she entered the dining room. April slowly strolled behind her.

"Mom, do weee . . ." Grace cleared her throat to stop her voice from cracking. "Do we have any juice?" She looked at the refrigerator.

"Oh, yes. Would you girls like some?" Her mother turned around and walked farther into the kitchen, with Grace behind her. As her mother turned her back, Grace whipped around to look at April. Wide-eyed, she dramatically pointed toward the purse on the dining room table.

April narrowed her eyes on the bag. Her heart thumped harder and harder with each step she took. She straightened out her glasses and closed her mouth. Her lips were chapped from breathing through her mouth. She swallowed hard. She licked her lips. April opened the purse.

Please, oh please let it be where Grace said it would be . . . Is it here? Side pocket, right?

April heard Grace and her mother talking in the kitchen.

"Yes, please," Grace said, standing right behind her mother.

Her mother opened the refrigerator. "Would you like apple or white grape?"

"Ummm. I don't know. Uh, oh yeah, and can April sleep over?"

"Did you ask your mom if you can sleep over, April?" April heard Mrs. Galapagos ask loudly.

"OH! I'll take WHITE GRAPE and um . . . April is apple's favorite. I mean, I mean, apple is April's favorite." Grace chuckled.

"Uh, ok."

April heard the refrigerator door close. She heard footsteps coming back toward the dining room.

"April did you talk to your mo—"

"Oh, Mom! Can, um, can we, um . . ." Grace muttered.

The footsteps stopped. "Sweetie, are you okay?" April heard Mrs. Galapagos ask.

"Yes . . . yes . . . I'm fine," Grace said nervously.

"YEP!" April jumped into the doorway so they both could see her, a smile plastered on her face. "I asked my mom. She said 'yes' as long as you say okay."

Grace smiled back and took the juice boxes from her mom's hands. "Thanks, Mom. So, can she? Please, please, please?"

"Sure," her mother said, bending down to give Grace a kiss on her forehead.

"Thanks!" said Grace.

The girls ran up the stairs, into Grace's room, and closed the door behind them.

FOURTEEN

THE GIRLS were both breathing heavily from running up the stairs. "I . . . got it," April panted. She bent over to pull up the leg of her jeans and slid down her pink sock. She grabbed the phone and stood up.

"Ta-da!" She tried to smile and catch her breath at the same time. "How awesome . . . am I?"

Grace took the phone. "OK . . . fingers crossed that this works."

April crossed her pointer and middle finger, then her ring finger and pinky. "Yep."

"Hi Abbey," said Grace as she texted, "can April and Austin stay over for pizza and a sleepover?" Grace hit *send*.

Each time April blinked felt like an eternity. They stared at the phone. *Silence.*

Grace swallowed. "Ya know, Eve's grandma may be right."

"'Bout what? Having a gift?"

"Yep. I mean . . . remember the door? You may be able to do other stuff. Like last week when my dress was tucked into my tights by accident after I left the bathroom. 'Member that?"

April smirked. *Don't laugh. Don't laugh. She was SO traumatized.*

Grace continued, "Do you know how many kids screamed 'fail' and 'loser'? I seriously wished I were invisible. But, as much as I wished for it—*nada*! But YOU wanted the door to close, and you did it. You wanted Austin to stop picking on you and . . . POOF!" Grace threw her arms in the air. "Now he is smaller than my grandmother's mop. And, you turned on your fan in your bedroom just by thinking about it." She ended her speech by putting her hands on her hips and nodding her head.

"Ok . . ." April wiped her sweaty hand on her pants. "But, I don't want to get into a mess like this again."

"I know. But, think about what WE could do," Grace said, smiling.

"We?"

"Yeah! You, me, and Eve can fix stuff." Her smile stretched from ear to ear.

"What kind of stuff?" April asked.

"I don't know . . . uh . . . we could make sure all the puppies at the pound get a home. Uh . . . we . . . could . . . Oh! You could get Ms. Meanie back for giving you that detention. You could make her come to school looking like a clown. Imagine it! Her makeup painted all over her face."

They both laughed.

"But, what if something goes wrong again?" April asked.

"We'll have Eve's book," said Grace. "What else could possibly go wrong?"

FIFTEEN

*D*ING. *D*ING.

April looked down at the bed. She saw she had a text message and quickly picked up her phone.

She read aloud, *"Sure honey. See you tomorrow.* YES!" April threw back her head.

"Cool. Now text her and ask if Eve can come over tomorrow morning."

"Yes, yes," April said, feverishly texting and focused.

Thx Mom! Can a new friend Eve come over 4 a playdate in the morning? <3

Buzz. Buzz.

"Oh your mother texted back," Grace said, opening the message on Mrs. Galapagos's phone and showing it to April.

Sure Rita. If you want, I will take the next sleepover. ☺

"YES!" Grace and April screamed. They jumped up and down.

BAM! The front door slammed.

"Girls! Come on downstairs. Pizza's here," Grace's mother yelled up the stairs.

Boom, Boom, BOOM, BOOM. Someone was running up the stairs. April and Grace looked at each other.

"Oh no, Michael's home," Grace said.

Michael swung the door open. *WHACK!* It slammed against the wall.

"Awesome. Two of you to bother tonight." His evil grin grew.

"MOM! Michael is bothering us!" Grace screamed.

April stared at the closet door. *Oh no. Austin, please don't make a sound.*

"Arrr. Arrr."

Michael looked around the room. "What's that?"

Grace walked over to the closet door and stood in front of it. "MOOOOOOMM! Michael is in MY room bothering us!" she screamed again.

"Michael, leave your sister alone!" Grace's mom yelled. "Everyone come downstairs NOW and wash your hands."

"What's that?" Michael said, looking at the bed.

Oh no! I have to do something. Michael can't get the phone then he will know. He'll get us in more trouble than we are already in.

April grabbed the phone. "It's my phone." She busily pressed buttons on the phone, opening the text messages.

Delete message: Yes.

Michael snatched it from her hands.

"No it's not—this is Mom's phone. What are you guys doing with Mom's phone?" He glared at both girls, then looked at the phone. "What are you two doing?"

"Arrr. Arrr!"

April swallowed. She wiped her hands on her pants again. "I thought it was my phone. Oops. It looks just like my phone . . . SEE . . ." She picked up her phone from the bed. She waved it in the air. It was the same kind of phone as Mrs. Galapagos had.

Michael pursed his lips and narrowed his eyes. "What is that sound?" He looked at the closet door and Grace standing in front of it.

"MOM! Can you come get Michael? He won't leave my room!" Grace whined. April started biting her lower lip nervously.

Grace's mom stomped up the stairs. "I am tired of you two always bickering!"

Michael raced out of her room. Running behind him, Grace followed.

He pointed at Grace. "Mom, they had your phone. I think they're up to something. And, I heard this—"

"Mom," Grace interrupted, "April accidentally picked up your phone 'cause she thought it was hers." She pushed Michael's hand down out of her face.

April jumped in to stop Michael finishing what he was going to say. "Our phones look alike Mrs.—"

"Fine, fine, fine. Everyone downstairs. It's time for dinner. NOW!" Mrs. Galapagos pointed down the stairs, and took the phone from Michael.

As they walked downstairs, April whispered to Grace, "I deleted it."

April and Grace exhaled a sigh of relief. And, Grace smiled.

SIXTEEN

AFTER PIZZA, they all watched a movie in the den. The girls got ready for bedtime in Grace's room. Grace's mom helped them pull out and make the rollaway bed.

After Mrs. Galapagos left the room, April looked at her phone.

"Yessssss!" April put the phone on Grace's computer desk.

"What?" Grace asked.

"My mom said Eve can come over tomorrow morning." They high-fived.

April opened the closet door. The little white dog was curled up on the closet floor, sleeping.

"Night, night Austin. This was a long day for you, too." She pulled out a small piece of pizza from her pocket in her jeans that she had wrapped in a napkin at dinner. She placed it on the ground next to him.

"I promise to fix this tomorrow. I love you," April whispered. She closed the closet door and climbed into the rollaway bed. She fell fast asleep.

The next thing she heard was, "Arf. Arf. Arrrr . . ."

April jumped up. She could see through the window that the sun was starting to come out. Austin was quietly barking and whining in the closet. She opened the closet door.

"What?"

The little white dog jumped up and down.

"What is wrong with you?" April whispered.

He ran across Grace's shoes. "Arrr . . ."

He ran in circles in the closet. "Arr . . ."

April put her hands on her hips. She tipped her head to the side. "Why are you whining?"

"He has to go to the ba . . ." Grace mumbled with her face in the pillow.

"He has to *what*?" April asked, throwing her arms in the air. Austin started jumping up and down again.

Grace lifted her head. "He has to go to the bathroom." Her hair was stuck to the side of her face, and her eyes were still closed. *Flop!* She dropped her head back onto the pillow.

The little dog ran over to Grace, jumped on the bed, and gave her a big lick. "Ewww," she said and wiped her face. She rolled over to the other side of the bed and knocked the dog onto the floor.

He grunted.

April chuckled.

"Not funny," Grace muttered.

April took off the pajamas she had borrowed from Grace, and put on the jeans and shirt she had worn on Friday. April unzipped the backpack. Austin jumped right in. She zipped it up. She wrinkled her nose. "Geez, Austin, you even smell like a dog."

"Grrrr . . ."

She put the backpack on her back, and pushed the cell phone into her pocket. Austin kept wiggling from side to side in the bag.

Move faster, move faster. The last thing I need is dog pee in my backpack. Ewww! Or even worse, leaking through the backpack onto me.

She poked Grace's shoulder. "Grace. Grace, wake up."

"I haven't gone back to sleep," Grace croaked.

"Ha, you sound like Michael. Hello, I'm Grace, but I sound like a boy," April said, making her voice deep to mock Grace.

Grace glared at her. Still smiling, April said, "I'm taking Austin outside to go to the bathroom. Meet me at my house in a few minutes."

"Yep."

"See you in a little bit." As April slowly opened the bedroom door, she saw Michael's door was still closed. Sunlight filled the hallway. She walked down the stairs. *Creak, creak, creak.* She got to the bottom and looked back up the stairs.

Whew, I didn't wake anyone.

Austin's movements were becoming faster in the bag.

"Stay still, Austin," she said over her shoulder to the backpack.

"April, who are you talking to?" said a voice from the den.

April's heart started to race as she saw Grace's dad in the den reading the newspaper. She swallowed. "Oh, uh, no one," she laughed.

Austin kept wiggling and moving in the backpack. She turned to face Mr. Galapagos so he could not see the moving bag. "I was just thinking about the chores I have to do when I get home. I want to go get them done so . . . um . . . that's right, so Eve—a new friend of Grace's and mine—can come over to hang out."

He raised an eyebrow. April gave a broad smile.

"Ok. I'll message your dad that you are coming back home," he said, reaching for his cell phone. He started texting.

Get outta here. Move quickly, but don't let him see the bag.

"Arrr . . ."

Austin whined and wiggled some more.

Austin is going to burst . . . all over my back.

"Ok. Thanks, Mr. Galapagos." April scurried sideways out the front door. She closed it behind her, and took off running up the street, away from her house.

SEVENTEEN

BRIGHT sunlight covered the street. But, April was the only one outside at 7am on a Saturday morning. Just before the corner, there was a small park.

"Austin . . ." she said, breathing heavily, "we're here!" She took the book bag off and put it on the ground. She quickly unzipped it and took the little white dog out. She placed him on the grass and looked in the bag.

"All clear—no pee or poo."

He trotted a few steps and started to go to the bathroom.

"Wow, you really did have to go. It sounds like a hose," she said.

He looked up at her and growled.

"Sorry . . . sorry," she said. "I'll give you privacy." April looked up at the white, puffy clouds. The morning sun warmed her cheeks and made her close her eyes.

Austin is fluffy like those clouds. Ha ha. I could just imagine him floating off like a cloud . . .

"ARRRR! ARRRR!"

Austin let out a loud whine—almost a scream. She opened her eyes to find him two feet off the ground and floating higher, just like the clouds she was imagining. She wrapped both of her hands firmly around him and pulled him close to her chest. *I just made him float.*

He floated like a cloud like my daydream. I am a witch. Wow. I am . . . a . . . witch.

"Oh my, Austin, I am so sorry!"

He grumbled.

"I'll let you finish what you were doing. I promise I won't think about you floating into the sky anymore. I won't interrupt you again . . ." She looked back at the morning sky and closed her eyes.

OMG . . . Am I a witch? Maybe I do have a gift. But, is this a blessing or a curse? What if mean people try to make me do mean spells like in the movies? Geez, what if I hadn't opened my eyes? Poor Austin would have floated to heaven. April took a deep breath. *But, hmmm . . . what else I can do?*

"Ewwwww!" April wrinkled her nose. "Austin I think I smell what you are doing now."

"Grrr . . ."

"I'm not looking. I'm not looking." She kept her eyes closed.

Maybe this is a blessing. Maybe Grace is right. Eve's book may help. Then, I won't make any more messes. Gee, we really could do some great stuff. She laughed as she imagined Ms. Meanie with clown face paint. *And, I could save that worm that Jimmie was poking with a stick. I could make the worm wiggle away too fast for Jimmie to catch it.* Or better yet, she could make it jump into his nose. She laughed again.

"Hey! Sleeping Beauty!"

April opened her eyes. She saw Grace looking at her from the sidewalk at the edge of the park.

"Austin and I were waiting for you to wake up," Grace said, pointing to the dog. Austin sat, with his head titled to the side, looking at April.

Grace held her cell phone up. "Eve said she is on her way."

"Oh my goodness, we'd better get back now. I was, uh, daydreaming."

In a rush, April scooped up Austin and placed him in the backpack, giving him one last pet before she zipped it up.

Grace pinched her nose. "Oh my! He really did have to go."

April put on the backpack and stood up.

"What about that?" Grace said, pointing to Austin's pile of poo.

"I didn't bring a bag," April said, walking toward her house.

"But—"

April turned and talked to Grace while walking backward. "I'll come back later and get it. We have to go. I have to tell you what just— whoa." April tripped but caught herself before she fell. "That was close."

As they walked in the door of April's house, they saw her mom watching the news.

"Hi girls," she said, looking at the clock. "Wow! You're up and out early."

"Yes . . . um . . ." April said, looking at Grace.

"Yeah, we want to finish our project with our new friend, Eve," Grace said.

"I thought it was an essay," April's mom said.

"Oh, yeah, it is. It's a group project that's an essay on the president," April said, bumping Grace.

April's heart pounded. Her mouth was open, but no words were coming out.

"We took some books out of the school library," Grace said, looking at the backpack.

Knock. Knock. Knock.

"That must be Eve," Grace said. April glanced at the clock and she opened the door.

Perfect timing, Eve. Thank you.

EIGHTEEN

*B*REATHE. *Focus. Austin doesn't normally get up until 10—at the earliest. Fingers crossed. Mom won't worry about him until lunchtime. We should have this fixed by then. Hopefully.*

Eve stood at the door next to her mother. She had on a pretty, white shirt with a pink design on it and jeans.

"Good morning!" Eve said, smiling. She pushed a container into Grace's hands. "My mom made them. These are beignets." Eve smiled and looked at her mom. Her mother was looking into the house.

"*Ben-yays?*" April said, lifting the container's lid. The donut-like pastries made her mouth water.

Yum . . . powdered sugar AND fried dough. *Wow, this is better than the stuff at the carnival.*

Just as April was about to reach in for one, her mother appeared behind her.

"Oh! Beignets!" April's mom said, lifting the container out of April's hands. "I love beignets. Come in, come in." She motioned Eve and her mother inside.

Eve's mother extended her arm to April's mother. "My name is Edna. Edna LaRue."

"I'm Abbey—Abigail Appleton." April's mother shook Eve's mother's hand, then looked at Eve. "And, you must be Eve."

"Yes, ma'am. Pleased to meet you." Eve smiled.

"Come on, Eve. Let's go upstairs to work on the essay," April said, winking at her.

"Essay? What essay?" Mrs. LaRue asked Eve. "I thought you were just coming over to play?"

Eve's eyes grew wide. She stood there not blinking, looking at her mother.

"Oh, we asked Eve if she wanted to join our project group," Grace said to Mrs. LaRue. "In school, we picked groups to write an essay and give a presentation. And, um . . ."

"Yes!" Eve said excited. "Oh, yes, I would . . . um . . . love to join your group."

ACHOO!! ACHOO!! ACHOO!!

"God bless you, Abbey," said Mrs. LaRue.

ACHOO!!! ACHOO!!! ACHOO!!!

"Bless you, Mom." April felt her lip quiver. Blood rushed to her cheeks.

Oh no! Oh no! I have to get Austin upstairs. I don't want her to get sick. Oh gosh, I am the suckiest daughter. She darted over to the tissue box and brought it to her mother.

"Gee, I only sneeze like this around animals."

"OK, we'd better go get started." April firmly grabbed Eve's hand and they ran up the stairs.

"We . . . made it," Grace panted as they entered April's room.

"I . . . thought . . . for sure, we were going to get caught," April said, hunched with her hands on her knees as she gasped for air.

Oh! Austin. Gosh, he probably is burning up in there.

She placed the book bag on the floor. Then she looked up at the open bedroom door.

Oh crud! I forgot to close the door. Ugh, I wish it would just close again.

And, before their eyes, as April slowly took Austin out of the book bag, the door did just that.

NINETEEN

"YOU DID** that again, didn't you?"** Grace asked, looking at April.

April stared at the door. "Uh . . . yeah . . ."

"That is super cool, BUT super creepy at the same time."

"So, I bet that keeps happening?" Eve said, smirking and looking at April's walls.

"And, I . . . uh . . . sorta made Austin float when we were at the park."

"What!" Grace's jaw dropped.

"Well . . . I really did make him float up, uh, higher and higher. I thought about how he looks like a cloud. You know, because he's white and fluffy. So he started to float up . . . toward the sky. But, I caught him before he drifted too high."

Austin grumbled. Grace's mouth was still open.

"I . . . I . . . I don't know what's happening." April looked down at the rug. Her glasses slid down her nose. She pushed them back up.

Eve cleared her throat. "Your room is so pretty. Pink is my favorite color."

April picked her head up to look at Eve. "I picked the brightest pink I could find in the store."

"I love the glitter, and the beads remind me of New Orleans," Eve said, looking at the block lettering on the wall that said A-P-R-I-L outlined with brightly colored glitter and different colored beads. Eve touched the beads. "I like bright colors, too."

"Oh, you would love these jeans I have then." April took a pair of rainbow-striped jeans out of her dresser.

"Oh, aren't those the bee's knees!" Eve said.

"Huh?" April tipped her head to the side.

"Oh, yeah, that's just something my mom says. It means . . . uh . . . like . . . aren't those great. You know what I mean?" Eve gave a shy smile.

April laughed. "I get it."

"OK, girls. Let's stop the fashion show and start working," Grace said, giving a little attitude.

"Ok, *Gracie.*" April rolled her eyes. Grace glared at her. She hated being called Gracie.

"Oh, yeah," Eve said, putting her book bag on the ground. She unzipped it and, with her teeth pressed together, grunted "Uh, uh," as she tried to pull out the biggest book ever.

Grace sat on the floor next to Eve. "Let me help." They both pulled . . . *FLOP!*

Achoo! Grace quietly sneezed.

"I know. It's SO dusty," Eve said, wiping the hard brown leather-bound book with her hand.

Grace opened the book. "The cover is so rough and heavy."

"What does that say?" April asked, putting one knee down on the ground.

'Choo . . . Austin sneezed. He shook his head around as if the dust were bothering him, too. He trotted under April's bed.

April looked under the bed. He had collapsed in the far corner. "Still have allergies as a dog, huh?" He was using his paw to rub and cover his nose. Then, she leaned in between Grace and Eve who were looking at the book. April closed the heavy front cover and ran her hand over the raised, braided trim. The edges were so bulky and hard. "It looks like a picture frame, but it feels sorta like leather and the snake skin from science class."

She ran her pointer finger across the large black letters on the cover that spelled *Magie*. "What is that? What does 'Maggie' mean?" April asked.

"It's 'mah-gee' not Maggie. And *magie* means 'magic' in French," Eve said, opening the book.

"Girls."

They froze as April's bedroom door opened. They slowly turned to see April's mom in the doorway with Eve's mom standing behind her.

OMG! OMG! Please, oh please, I hope we're creating a wall in front of this book. What if Eve's mom asks why she brought it over? Oh crud—Austin! Oh Austin, please stay under the bed . . . please, please, please . . .

TWENTY

"GIRLS, Mrs. LaRue is going to run a few errands, then she'll come back to pick up . . . are you okay?" Mrs. Appleton eyes widened as she looked at April. "Honey, you are as pale as a ghost."

April swallowed. She slid closer to Eve and Grace.

Please don't let them see the book. Please

don't let them see the book. Please Austin, stay under the bed.

"Oh no. I'm fine. We're just working on our essay."

Eve's mother poked her head into the room. "Eve honey, I'll be back in a couple of hours. Call me on my cell if you need me, ok?"

Eve could not speak. Grace lightly nudged her. Eve nodded her head up and down.

"Was Austin up yet when you girls left?" Mrs. Appleton asked, looking at April.

April held her breath. "Uh . . ."

"They were still sleeping. I think they stayed up later then we did playing, um, that new video game," Grace said, not blinking, with a big smile on her face.

"Oh, boys!" Mrs. Appleton said, looking at Mrs. LaRue. "Ok. If you girls need anything, I'll be downstairs." She closed the door. She and Eve's mother kept talking as they walked down the stairs.

April collapsed to the floor. "OMG, how come we didn't hear them coming?"

"We were all staring at the book." Grace turned the pages, making a rustling sound.

April sat back up. "Oh, yeah."

Grace wiggled her nose. "The pages smell like the reference section at the library. You know—the old library smell."

"They are almost as thin as tissue paper. They kind of feel like the old newspaper Mom used to wrap the dishes Nana gave her that are in the basement."

April looked closer at the old pages. She rubbed the slightly torn edges of the first few pages between her fingers. "They look like they were once white but—"

"Arrr . . ." Austin started to cry.

"What is that?" Eve asked. The girls peered under the bed.

Austin flopped onto his side with his legs stretched out. "Umph," he sighed with his mouth open. His tongue lay limp on the rug.

"Awww. He is so cute. You sure you don't want to keep him like this?" Eve asked, reaching her hand out to pet him.

Austin's eyes narrowed as he let out a growl.

"Sorry, sorry." Eve pulled her hand away from him. "You're just a cute little doggie . . . that looks, uh, hungry or, uh, thirsty—"

"Oh, crud! I'll get him some water," April jumped up. She went into the bathroom, which was next to her room. She grabbed the cup she used to rinse out her mouth after she brushed her teeth.

Perfect. Eww, I don't want a dog drinking

out of my cup. Maybe I should use his cup. It's his, uh, mouth.

She put her cup back onto the sink counter and picked up his. She filled it with water, then hurried back to her bedroom.

Door, please open.

It opened. She walked through.

Door, please close quietly. It gently closed. Eve and Grace stared with their mouths open. *This really is getting fun.*

"Close your mouths. My nana says, 'You may choke on a fly that way.'" April chuckled as she set the water down in front of Austin who was still under the bed.

"OMG . . . you really may be a witch." Grace shook her head, and returned to looking at the book. "So . . ." She raised her eyebrows. "How did you get this big, old book out without your parents seeing you?"

Eve smirked again. "My mom was watching

one of her DVR'd shows. And, Dad was still at work," she explained. "My mom doesn't hear anything when she's into one of her shows."

They all laughed.

"Ok. Give me a minute. I have to find that spell again," Eve said.

The girls were silent. They looked over Eve's shoulders at the fancy French lettering. Each turn of a page crackled and let out the scent of old-book-plus-basement.

"What does it say?" April asked. "What do those symbols mean?"

Eve did not reply. She continued to mumble quietly to herself.

"Eve? Eve?" Grace asked, staring at Eve's face.

"Give . . . me . . . another . . . second . . . AH HA!" Eve exclaimed. "I've got it! Your brother will be back to normal in just a few easy . . ." Eve's eyes stayed focused on the page. "Well . . ."

her voice raised an octave. "Well, maybe not easy for . . . um, you." Eve bit her lower lip as she looked at April.

"Huh?" April looked over the top of her glasses. "What do you mean not easy for *me*?"

TWENTY-ONE

"WELL, UM, let's just start with the first step, ok?" said Eve. "Sorry, about the zoning out. My French is ok, but I have to focus. I don't read it very fast. April, what is your brother's favorite drink?"

"Oh, that's a no-brainer! Chocolate milk."

"OK! Can you go get some chocolate milk?"

"Ok, ok, ok," April said, trying to convince herself this would be easy. "But, what if Mom asks me something about you-know-who?" She angled her head in Austin's direction. He was still busily licking up the water.

"Don't forget, we said earlier that they were up late playing that new video game. Just say that he's still sleeping. We both know he AND Michael sleep really late." Grace looked at the clock. "It's not even ten yet." Grace pointed at the clock, which read 9:42am.

"Yeah, I can do that. I want to fix this," April dropped her shoulders, pushed out her chest, and took a deep breath. "I AM going to fix this."

Austin finally stopped drinking. He grumbled.

"I know, I know. I said that before. This will work . . . this time. I'm sure." April bent her body forward, looking under the bed. "Stay here. I'll be right back."

She zoomed downstairs and zipped past the front door. She saw her father in the living room watching TV. She held her breath and whizzed through the dining room to the kitchen. She saw her mother and exhaled.

Ok. I can do this. Remember: video games late and they usually sleep late.

"Hey, kiddo," her mother said.

"Mom, can I have some chocolate milk?"

"Sure honey. Usually that is your brother's favorite. I wonder when Austin is . . ." *ACHOO!!!*

April's heart beat faster. "Bless you, Mom," she said, handing her a tissue from the counter.

I just need the chocolate milk. I gotta get outta here. April looked into her mother's eyes, which were watering and red. *Geez! I am making her sick, I dehydrated poor Austin, not to mention turned him into a dog over these stupid glasses . . . Geez.*

"Thank you, honey." Mrs. Appleton smiled at April. "What was I saying again?"

"This is, uh, for . . . Eve."

Breathe. Just breathe. The faster I get this done, the faster Mom will feel better, and Austin will be back to normal.

Her mom sneezed again. She rubbed her eyes.

"Bless you, Mom. Are you ok?"

Her mother washed her hands. Then, she took a cup out of the cabinet.

"Yes. But my allergies are bothering me. Honey, have you been around any animals?"

April slowly took a step away from her mom. She shook her head.

Oh no! I am horrible. She never lied to her mother, and now she had lied to her twice in one weekend. She had to get upstairs ASAP.

Her mother poured the chocolate syrup into the cup. She added the milk, stirred, and handed the glass to April.

"Thank you, Mom."

OK. Act normal. But get upstairs fast.

"Uh . . . ok . . . bye." She began to leave.

"Honey?"

She held her breath and turned around to face her mother.

"Do you and Grace want some chocolate milk, too?"

April dropped her shoulders and exhaled. "Oh, ok, I'll take up two more cups and we'll all share." She smiled and took the two cups her mom handed her. "Bye, Mom."

Don't spill it. Don't spill it.

As she returned to her room, she heard Grace say, "April's NOT going to like that."

"What?" April asked, closing her door. "What am I not going to like?" Her stomach began to churn.

TWENTY-TWO

"OH . . . UH . . ."** Grace said. "Great. You got the chocolate milk."

"Great!" Eve said.

"YEP!" April said with a smile. She placed the chocolate milk and cups on the dresser. "So . . . what am I not going to like?"

Grace leaned forward. "April?"

"Yes, Grace . . ." April raised one eyebrow as she looked at Grace.

"OK . . . you are not going to like the next

step. But . . . uh . . . think about . . . getting Austin back to normal . . . ok?" Grace said, grinning.

"Now . . . go get a used piece of Austin's clothing," Eve instructed.

April raised one eyebrow. She looked at the book, then back at Eve. "Why? His room is disgusting. And his clothes are even grosser!"

"Well, the next step *is* a little gross." Eve said, the pitch of her voice rising again. "It has to be a used article of clothing because it has his scent on it. Then, you have to cut three small squares off the used piece of clothing—"

April wrinkled up her nose. "You want me to actually touch his dirty clothes?"

"That's not the gross part," Eve said, trying to smile.

"*Not* the gross part? What?"

"You have to mix the clothes into the drink—"

"Huh?" April tilted her head to the side.

"Well . . . you have to stir the used clothing into the chocolate milk," Eve explained, "and then . . . you have to drink it."

April's heart sank. Blood rushed to her cheeks. She looked at Austin under the bed.

His eyes look so sad. Ok, ok. I made this mess. I have to fix it. Just get it done!

"I'm doing this for you." She took a deep breath then calmly stood up. "OK. I have to go to his room. I'll be right back . . ."

She tiptoed down the hall to Austin's room. She opened his door. *OMG, it smells like dirty feet in here. I can't believe I have to do this.*

She looked at the piles of clothes on the floor.

What is the least gross thing in here? Eww. Not that.

She moved one of his socks with her foot.

I have to find something.

She saw a pair of pants.

Eww. Not those. I think those are grass stains from practice. The clock is ticking. Find something, find something.

She looked to the left and to the right. She scanned the entire room then—*BINGO!*

Is this his winter hat? I think this is the only kinda clean thing in here.

She picked up the blue cotton hat and pushed it into her pocket. She quickly and quietly ran back down the hall and into her room, closing the door behind her.

"OK . . ." she said, breathing heavily. "I got it."

"What did you get?" Grace asked.

April leaned over and put her hands on her knees. With her heart thumping, she pulled the hat out of her pocket.

"Catch your breath, April," Eve said.

April closed her eyes. She inhaled then exhaled. "OK . . . I'm ready," she said firmly.

"Ok. Mix the three hat squares with the chocolate milk," Eve directed. "Stir it around before you drink."

April looked at her bookshelf. On top of it was a cup with pens, pencils, markers, and a pair of scissors. As she cut three squares from the hat, Austin growled. "Oh, stop it! I'm sure there's another hat in that pigsty. Seriously, Austin, I am trying to fix this. Don't you want to be normal again?"

Grace looked at Austin, then back at April. "You know he can't answer you, right?"

April glared at Grace above the rim of her glasses. "He answers me . . . in his own way."

She put the hat squares into the cup of chocolate milk. She slowly stirred it using her finger. The navy blue hat turned an icky grey.

The mixture became soapy with little bubbles that grew bigger and bigger, increasing in size until they reached the very top of the cup.

"Wow. I think you just made a potion," Grace said.

April's eyes stayed fixed on the cup. She grabbed her stomach. "This is the grossest thing in the whole world."

"Sorry . . . but you have to . . . uh . . . drink ALL of it." Eve gulped.

The blood rushed from April's face.

"I'm sorry, April. This is the hard part," Eve said.

This is super gross. He plays sports. He sweats . . . a lot. Who knows how long this was on his floor? But, I have to do this. This is the only way to bring him back and to make sure my parents don't kill me. She glanced at the clock. *OMG, it is 10:15. Mom and Dad will start to worry, or even worse—call Grace's parents.*

April pinched her nose. She put the cup to her lips. She swallowed.

Don't puke, don't puke.

She swallowed again.

TWENTY-THREE

OH NO, I think I am going to puke.

April finished it, slammed the cup down on her desk, and burped loudly. "Oops . . . excuse me!" She covered her mouth. Eve and Grace laughed.

"What next? Do I have to go eat his dirty underwear now?"

"Don't be silly," Eve giggled. "THAT was the grossest part. Now to step two . . ."

"I am scared to ask," said April. "What is step two?"

Grace grinned. "This part may be fun!"

"I need you to pluck three hairs from Austin," Eve replied.

April let out a huge breath. She reached under the bed and gently pulled him out. Putting him on the bed, she sat next to him. "OK, Austin."

"Grrr . . ." Austin growled.

"Do you want to stay a dog?" He stopped. "I'll do it fast, k?"

Austin growled again.

"Austin, I'm sorry. I know you hate me. I'd hate me, too." She looked down at him. She brushed her hand over his head and down his back. Then, she petted him again.

She held Austin down on the bed with one hand, and quickly pulled a strand of fur from his head.

"Arrrr!" He jumped straight up.

"Lie down, Austin," April begged. "I have to get two more hairs from you for the spell."

Austin scurried to the end of the bed. He jumped off. He ran in a circle. Looking dizzy, he slammed into the door.

BAM! He flopped to the floor.

April and Eve laughed.

"Shhhh," Grace giggled. "I don't know which looked more painful, the hair pulling or the head-on collision with the door."

"What is going on? Are you okay?" April's mother yelled up the stairs.

Oh no. What should I do? I have to tell Mom something so she stays downstairs.

April picked up one of the empty cups and zoomed over to Austin. She scooped him up, placed him on the bed, and dropped the hair.

Crud! I lost it. Oh well. The bed should be a little more comfortable to lie on while he wakes back up. Please let him be okay. I hope that didn't cause permanent damage.

She paused. She relaxed her shoulders and took a deep breath.

Be calm. Act normal.

April went out the door to the stairs. "Hey Mom," she said, smiling down at her mother at the bottom of the stairs. "Sorry about that. I . . . uh . . . dropped the empty cup." She held it up to show her mom and flashed a wide smile. "That was great chocolate milk. Thank you!"

"I just wanted to make sure you are OK," Mrs. Appleton said. "Call me if you girls need anything."

April ran back into her room and shut the door. She leaned her back against it and looked at the clock.

It's already 10:30! Oh no, oh no.

"You're right!" Eve was saying to Grace. "We could do super cool spells and stuff."

"I know. Between April and your book we could—"

They stopped talking when they saw April.

Austin opened his eyes. He was trying to hold up his wobbly head but gave up, letting it flop back onto the bed. April sat down next to him.

"One . . . two . . . three." She plucked three strands of fur from his body.

"Arr! Arr! Arr!" Austin yelped.

"He's just a little mixed up right now," Eve said. "He ran into the door super fast."

"I got them!" April said.

TWENTY-FOUR

"**E**VE, what do I do with these?" April asked.

"We're at the last step. Put him in the closet. Make sure the light is off in there."

Austin lifted his head. His eyes bulged and wobbled from side to side.

"He looks a bit better," laughed Grace. "We want him to come back in one piece."

April picked him up and opened the closet.

"Make sure there's nothing on the ground,"

said Eve, as she tried to crane her neck to look into the closet from her seated position.

April bent over. With her empty hand, she threw everything out of the closet that was on the floor. All of her shoes, a few purses, and a belt flew through the air.

Out of breath, she stood up straight. "Ok, what now? I'm tired."

"I know. I'm getting tired just watching you," Grace said. She and Eve laughed.

"Ha, ha. A joke from the girls who are just sitting there," April said, pointing to them on the carpet.

"Sorry. We're almost done," Eve said calmly.

April's glasses slid down her nose, which was damp with sweat. She pushed them back up.

She took three big breaths. "OK. I feel a little better."

"Uh . . . April?" Eve asked quietly.

"Yes?"

"Can you wipe off the closet floor?" Eve asked.

"What! *Why?*" April said, sighing.

"Well, the spell says the floor should be clean. I don't want it to not work because of that small thing."

"Fine." April put Austin back on the bed. She placed the three hairs on her desk.

She ran back into the bathroom she and Austin shared. She grabbed the sponge her mom and dad used to clean the tub. She turned on the water and rinsed it out. Adding a little soap, she ran back to her room and closed the door.

She fell to her knees and quickly wiped off the closet floor. She looked at the bottom of the sponge.

"Ewww. It's black." She wrinkled her nose and threw the sponge behind her. It landed on top of one of the shoes she had just thrown out of the closet.

"It's clean now." April collapsed onto her bed next to Austin.

Please, oh please, let that be it. Witch or no witch, I'm exhausted. Oh . . . look at poor Austin. He looks so . . . hopeless. OK, I can do this.

"Just a little bit longer, and this nightmare will be behind us," April said to Austin.

"April," Eve asked, "are you ready?"

"Heck yeah!" April sat up. Her heart was still thumping.

"Last step," Eve said. "Yay! Put Austin on the closet floor. Close the door. Hold the hairs in your hand. Then say this:

"Heaven, please help with the recent past,
To undo the spell that I just cast.
Please take this request as formal,
And turn my brother back to normal."

TWENTY-FIVE

APRIL'S eyes widened. "Hey! That's what I said before."

"Really?" Eve asked.

"Yep," April said, proudly lifting up her chin. "I found it. It wasn't in a cool hundred-year-old book, but on Google."

"That's good. You were doing the right thing," Eve said, excited.

"Hmmm. Interesting," said Grace. "I couldn't find it on Google, but April could with the same keywords. And, the online spell is the same as the spell in your book—well, at least the words are the same. I wonder what witch put it online. And, how many other witches are there?" Grace pondered, looking off into the distance.

"Ok, Sherlock. Let's figure that out later. Right now, I have to worry about getting my brother back." April smiled, looking down at Austin. Austin tilted his head to the side. April felt like he was giving her a small smile.

April picked the hairs up from her desk. "Wish me luck!" she said, looking at her friends lying on the floor.

"Good luck," Eve and Grace said together. They both crossed their fingers.

April scooped Austin up from the bed with one hand. She whispered in his ear, "This will work."

She placed him on the clean closet floor. He

lay down, looking up at her. His eyes were wide and unblinking.

April held her breath with her eyes locked onto his. "Remember when I was super sick a few months ago with that really high fever? You even brought me soup in bed. You were so worried. Your eyes looked just like they do right now."

She could feel huge, tight knots in her stomach.

I think I may puke.

"My mother is going to call Grace's parents any minute now. Then, I will be in SO much trouble for—geez—everything."

I've run out of time. This is it. I'm starting to feel dizzy. Oh no. What if this doesn't work? Then Grace and Eve will get in trouble, too, for helping me. Then, I will be a bad friend, the worst daughter, and absolutely the most horrible sister in the entire world. April exhaled.

"Just breathe," Eve said, trying to give April a smile.

"April?" Grace asked. "You have to close the closet door."

"I know but, but, what if . . ."

"April, it will work because, as my *grandmère* said, 'Some people have gifts.'"

April took a breath. She looked at Eve. "You think I really have a gift? Do you really think I am a witch? You don't think that door thing was some weird, uh . . ."

"I know you have a gift," Eve said, smiling.

"Remember the floating dog thing, too?" Grace asked.

April smiled at her friends, but still felt jittery inside.

She wiped her sweaty palm on her pants. Smiling at Austin, she closed the closet door.

I promise if he is turned back, then I will not do anything like this to him again. I know I will

want to, but he doesn't deserve this. Yeah, he
may bother me, but, but he also protects me.

April closed her eyes.

She said, "*Heaven above, please help with
the recent past,*

To undo the spell that I just cast.

Please take this request as formal,

And turn my brother back to normal."

And then she slowly opened the door.

TWENTY-SIX

WHEN April looked into the closet, she saw her angry, red-faced brother. His arms were tightly crossed. His dark brown hair was standing straight up on his head.

April gasped and put her hand over her mouth. *Uh oh. Maybe the run into the door caused some damage.* He looked like he had been struck by lightning and had a massive sunburn.

She dropped her hands and jumped on him. She hugged him so tightly.

He pushed her off. "I cannot believe you did that to me!" he yelled.

"Austin, I'm sorry," April pleaded.

"I don't want to hear it!" he said. Their mom always said that when they were in trouble. "I'm not going to tell Mom and Dad, but you are going to do all of my chores for the next month." He walked to her door.

"Wait, Austin!" she grabbed his arm.

"What!"

April slowly raised her eyes from the ground. "I guess I'm the 'Prankster of the Year' now." She lifted one corner of her mouth, giving Austin a half grin.

Austin's face was beet red. He narrowed his eyes and tightened his lips. "Now it's two months of chores." He forcefully turned the knob.

"Wait! Wait!" April said jumping up and down.

"What!" he said, his teeth clenched together.

"You have to sneak out, and then come in through the front door. Mom and Dad think you're at Michael's."

Austin glared at her, not even noticing the other girls. His tightly squeezed lips relaxed. "Fine. But, I don't have my book bag or overnight stuff."

"Just say you left everything at Michael's. I left my stuff there, too. Just say you'll pick it up later, you're tired, and you forgot."

"Fine. Go downstairs and watch out for me. I'll sneak out the door. Then, I'll come back in and slam it," he said. "And you can't let Mom and Dad know that you're doing my chores, either." He pointed his finger in her face.

That used to get April really angry. But, she quietly looked down at her feet. "OK. I promise."

"Hi, Austin. Nice to see you back with us," Grace said, giving an awkward smile.

Austin glanced at her and rolled his eyes.

"Austin? Be nice," April said. "They helped get you back to normal."

He glared at her again. She looked down at the rug and left her bedroom.

She loudly stomped down the stairs. Her parents were in the kitchen. "Ummm . . . Mom and Dad, can we have a snack?"

"Sure, princess," her dad answered.

"Can we have some—"

Bam! The front door slammed.

"Hello?" Austin asked from the hallway.

"We're in here!" April yelled.

"Great, you're home," their mom said with a smile. "I was getting ready to call Rita."

"This is a sleeping record for you, Austin," Mr. Appleton said, putting his hand on Austin's shoulder.

"I guess, uh . . ." Austin said, looking at April.

Oh no! Oh no! Austin, think. Think of something to say. We can't get caught now!

Austin stared at April. April swallowed hard.

April jumped in. "I thought you and Michael stayed up playing Michael's new video game." April had her eyes locked on Austin's.

"Well, yeah. We played it for a while. It was pretty late when we went to bed. But I guess, I was just, uh, tired," Austin said, smirking at April.

April smiled. They both looked at their mom and dad.

Mrs. Appleton opened the refrigerator. "Anyway, it's perfect timing. You kids ready for a snack?"

Grace and Eve came running down the stairs.

"Everyone go wash your hands then come sit—" *ACHOO!!!* "I wonder what is bothering my allergies. I'm usually only allergic to animals," Mrs. Appleton said, looking at April's father.

April, Austin, Eve, and Grace walked toward the bathroom, chuckling. They all looked at each other and smiled. Austin ran into the bathroom first. He slammed the door in the girls' faces.

Grace looked at April. "I guess everything is back to normal in Appleton-land?"

"I sure hope so," April said, letting out a huge breath. "Well, I will be up to my eyeballs in laundry and dishes. But it's better than what Mom and Dad would do to me—"

Austin came out of the bathroom. He quietly said to April, "You can start by cleaning my room tonight. You know Dad expects our rooms clean by the time we leave for Sunday dinner at Nana's. You may want to get a head start."

He walked away, chuckling to himself. Grace's eyes bulged. She pointed at Austin's back. She covered her mouth with one hand, so as to not let out a loud laugh. Eve and April started to laugh, looking at the little white chunks of dog hair stuck to the back of his shirt.

"OMG! OMG!" Grace said, laughing.

April closed her eyes. *I wish my new glasses were here right now.*

The doorbell rang. April's mother opened the door and the delivery man handed her a small package. April's mom looked at it. "April, your new glasses are here." Her mother walked into the kitchen with the package and began opening it.

"You just did that, huh?" Grace asked, wide-eyed.

"Yep," April smirked. "So, what are you guys doing next weekend?"

★ ABOUT THE AUTHOR ★

Talia Aikens-Nuñez is a children's book author specializing in bilingual and multicultural children's books. Her first book, *Escucha Means Listen*, was released in by Musa Publishing in 2012. *OMG . . . Am I A Witch?!* is Talia's first chapter book and she is working on finding a home for her next children's chapter book, *Dragon Guardians*. Talia lives with her husband, daughter and newborn son on a river in Connecticut.

CPSIA information can be obtained at www.ICGtesting.com
Printed in the USA
BVOW04s1754090414

350026BV00004B/5/P